Sixty Years Bridge Crossing Jubilee

Bridge Crossing Jubilee

By
Iesha Shaw

Table of Contents

Introduction

Civil Rights: What are civil rights?

The civil rights movement is vital to democracy. Regardless of color, religion, or other attributes, they are assurances of equal social opportunity and legal protection. The rights to public education, government services, a fair trial, and voting are a few examples. Civil rights are protected by proactive government action, frequently in the form of legislation, as opposed to civil freedoms, which are liberties secured by imposing restrictions on the government.

What is the origin of civil rights?

Civil rights must be granted and upheld by the state, in contrast to human rights or natural rights, which people obtain naturally—possibly from nature. As a result, they differ widely in terms of time, culture, and kind of government and frequently adopt societal norms that either tolerate or reject discriminatory practices. For instance, in several democracies, the civil rights of the LGBTQ population have just lately gained prominence in political discourse.

A civil rights movement: what is it?

When many people believe that civil rights enforcement is insufficient, a civil rights movement may arise to demand that the laws be applied equally and without prejudice.

What was the American civil rights movement?

African Americans were marginalized, leading to the American civil rights movement, which started in the 1950s and grew during the early 1960s. Marches, boycotts, and acts of civil disobedience like sit-ins were all part of this movement, which had its roots primarily in African American churches and colleges in the South. The majority of the work was done locally. Still, it had a significant national impact and served as a model for civil rights organizations that have since expanded worldwide.

1

History of Civil Rights Movements in The U.S

From 1954 until 1968, the United States saw the civil rights movement, which aimed to end legislated discrimination based on race, racial segregation, and exclusion. Although the movement gained its biggest legislative successes in the 1960s following years of demonstrations and community protests, it began in the late 19th century during the Reconstruction era. It found its contemporary roots in the 1940s. The social movement's main tactics of civil disobedience and peaceful protest secured greater protections for everyone's civil rights in federal legislation (Williams, 2014).

The Reconstruction Provisions to the United States Constitution extended liberation and constitutional privileges of citizenship to all African Americans, the majority of whom had recently been enslaved, following the American Civil War and the ensuing abolition of slavery in the 1860s. For a brief while, African-American men could vote and hold public office. However, as time went on, Black people's civil rights were progressively taken away from them, frequently as a result of the racist Jim Crow laws, and African Americans in the South faced ongoing violence and discrimination from white supremacists. African Americans made several attempts over the next century to protect their legal and civil rights, including the movement for Civil Rights (1865–1896) and the Civil Rights Campaign (1896–1954). The movement was typified by peaceful large-scale demonstrations and acts of civil disobedience in the wake of well-reported incidents like Emmett Till's lynching. These included "sit-ins" in Greensboro and Nashville, numerous acts of demonstrations during the rally in Birmingham, a march from Selma to Montgomery, and boycotts like the one against the Montgomery bus (Vann R. Newkirk II, 2017) "("Brown v. Board of education: Summary, ruling & impact," 2009)."

The Supreme Court ruled in 1954 that the legal foundations of legislation permitting racism and discrimination in the United States were unconstitutional, marking the pinnacle of an African American legal campaign. In landmark decisions against racist discrimination, the Warren Court established the separate but equal doctrine. These decisions outlawed segregation in public schools and other public spaces and overturned all state laws that prohibited interracial marriage. The segregationist Jim Crow laws that were common in the Southern states were eventually repealed in large part due to the verdicts (Ball & Horwitz, 2000).

Progressives in the movement collaborated with the U.S. Congress in the 1960s to pass several important federal laws authorizing the surveillance and execution of regulations pertaining to civil rights. Racial prejudice of any kind, including segregation in public places, companies, and schools, was outlawed by the Civil Rights Act of 1964. By allowing federal supervision of voter rolls and polls in areas where minority voter representation has historically lagged, the Voting Rights Act of 1965 safeguarded and reinstated the right to vote. Discrimination in the purchase or leasing of real estate was outlawed in 1968 by the Fair Housing Act "("Struggle for Civil Rights," 2023)."

African Americans resumed their political careers, and youth movements spread nationwide. A surge of black community riots and protests from 1964 to 1970 reduced white middle-class support but boosted backing from private foundations (Haines, 1995). Black leaders of the Black Power movement faced criticism for their cooperative approach and commitment to legalism and non-violence when the movement emerged in 1965 and persisted until 1975. Its founders pushed for the community's economic independence and legal equality. African Americans, who continued to endure discrimination in employment, housing, education, and politics despite significant progress toward civil rights since the movement's zenith in the mid-1960s, provided support for the Black Power movement.

Many popular depictions of the struggle for civil rights revolve around the distinctive leadership style and ideology of Martin Luther King Jr., who was awarded the Nobel Peace Prize in 1964 for using peaceful resistance to fight racial inequity. Some academics point out that the movement was too varied to be attributed to a single individual, group, or tactic (Tyson, 1998).

1. Martin Luther King Jr.

Birth Date: January 15, 1929

Death Date: April 4, 1968

One of the leading figures in the American civil rights movement, he advocated through nonviolent resistance to racial segregation, and he delivered his famous speech entitled "I Have a Dream" during the 1963 March on Washington.

In addition to being the undisputed leader of the non-violent Civil Rights Movement in the 1960s, Dr. Martin Luther King Jr. was one of the most adored and despised individuals of his era. From his participation in the 1955 Montgomery bus boycott until his tragic demise in 1968, King contributed to the movement's growth and morale-boosting message of non-violent change. Fairness and non-violence are two easy words that summarize Martin Luther King Jr.'s legacy.

King grew up in a family of activists. The 1920s Back To Africa Movement led by Marcus Garvey profoundly affected his father. His mother was the daughter of a prominent African American clergyman in Atlanta. King achieved academic excellence. At fifteen, he effortlessly passed through grade levels and enrolled at Morehouse College, his father's alma mater. He then continued his education at Crozer Theological Seminary, graduating with a Bachelor of Divinity. He met and wed Coretta Scott at Boston University while working on a doctoral degree. King took a position at the Dexter Street Baptist Church in Montgomery, Alabama, in 1955, following his graduation with a doctorate. King founded the SCLC, a body devoted to developing African Americans' rights, following his orchestration of the bus boycott. King planned a protest. There have been sixty unsolved explosions of African American residences and churches following the end of World War II (Carson, 2000).

Marches, sit-ins, and boycotts were held. Millions saw the footage on the broadcast when Bull Connor, the chief of the Birmingham police department, attacked the protestors with dogs and fire hoses. King was taken into custody. But King and his family got backing from all over the country and the globe. He made his well-known "I Have a Dream" address to millions in Washington, D.C., later in 1963.

Following the Civil Rights Act of 1964, King focused on Southern African Americans' voting registration. He organized a march in Selma, Alabama, 1965 to raise the state's African American voting turnout. King was taken into custody once more. Once more, the cops attacked the protestors. Billy clubs, tear gas, and cattle prods were used against the non-violent protesters. The majority of the public was in favor of King and the demonstrators. King finished the arduous march from Selma to the nation's capital of Montgomery after President Johnson finally gave the order for the National Forces to defend the protesters from attack. The voting rights legislation of 1965 was passed as a result of the events in Selma "("After the Dream: Black and white Southerners since 1965 (review")," 2011).

On April 4, 1968, shortly after sunrise, James Earl Ray shot King. Urban regions saw spontaneous violence explode as grieving people let loose with their anger over the death of their leader. **There were riots in numerous American cities.**

But his efforts were never forgotten by the globe. **In 1963, he was chosen "Man of the Year" by Time magazine.** Upon receiving the Nobel Peace Prize in 1964, he was hailed as "the initial individual in the occidental world to have demonstrated to us that a struggle can be undertaken without bloodshed." The highest honor an American civilian may receive, the prestigious Presidential Medal of Freedom, was given to him posthumously in 1977. His birthday was declared a national holiday in the 1980s, giving people in the US a chance to commemorate the two principles he devoted his life to upholding every year: impartiality and non-violence ("Martin Luther King Jr. [ushistory.org"]," n.d.).

2. Rosa Parks (1913—2005)

Born: February 4, 1913, Tuskegee, AL

Died: October 24, 2005 (age 92 years), Detroit, MI

When Rosa Parks declined to give out her seat to a white man on a bus in Montgomery, Alabama, in 1955, she played a significant role in the beginning of the civil rights movement in the US. The leaders of the local Black community were moved by her acts to plan the Montgomery Bus Boycott. Over a year and a half, when Rosa Parks unintentionally lost her employment, the boycott led by a youthful Rev. Dr. Martin Luther King Jr. ended only after the U.S. Supreme Court declared that bus discrimination was unlawful. Parks gained national recognition over the following fifty years as a symbol of bravery and decency in the fight to eradicate ingrained racial discrimination **("Other Rosa Parks: Now 73, Claudette Colvin was first to refuse to give up a seat on Montgomery bus"," 2013).**

Rosa Parks: Roots of Activism

Rosa, a seamstress, and Raymond rose to prominence in Montgomery's sizable African American population. Living side by side with white people in a city where segregation laws prevailed, however, was a daily source of frustration for Black people. They were only allowed to attend certain subpar schools, drink from designated water fountains, and check out books from the "Black" library. Rosa also entered the Montgomery chapter of the NAACP in December 1943. She took on the role of chapter secretary despite Raymond's earlier discouragement due to concerns for her safety. Edgar Daniel (E.D.) Nixon, the chapter president, and she collaborated closely. In addition to serving as President of the local chapter of the Brotherhood of Sleeping Car Porters union, Nixon was a railroad porter who was well-known in the community for supporting Black individuals seeking to become eligible for voting "("Rosa Parks: Bus boycott, civil rights & facts," 2009).

3. John Lewis

Date of Birth: February 21, 1940

Death Date: July 17, 2020

As chairman of the Student Nonviolent Coordinating Committee (SNCC), Lewis was a key figure in the civil rights movement, participating in events like the Freedom Rides and the Selma to Montgomery marches.

So towering was John Lewis in the American civil rights movement, revered for keeping up the call of non-violent protest and struggle for justice and equality. Born to sharecroppers in 1940 in Alabama, Lewis tasted for himself the awful irony that lay behind the Southern imprimatur of Jim Crow segregation (Seelye, 2020). With conditions that were initially so forbidding and discouraging, the parents finally fought against the existent conditions; that is, the bravery of Rosa Parks and Martin Luther King inspired Lewis from the beginning on the way of activism and advocacy.

Out of his hard commitment came fast-growing importance in the Student Non-violent Coordinating Committee (SNCC), as he became one of its central leaders at the time of the committee's first founding. From sit-ins to freedom rides, the structurally racist power structures of the United States were approached by Lewis with unbending fearlessness (Seelye, 2020). From being bludgeoned on the Edmund Pettus Bridge in 1965 to shouting his resolve to gain voting rights for African Americans, Lewis was part of the Selma to Montgomery march.

Lewis went on with his social change engagements throughout the years, one after the other that followed his time after SNCC. Whether at the forefront of the Voter Education Project or ensconced some years later in the U.S. House of Representatives, Lewis was always a soldier dedicated to the causes that marked his work: fighting for the rights of minorities and making people hear issues.

He received many distinctions throughout his life for his activism work, like the Presidential Medal of Freedom and the Martin Luther King Jr. Non-violent Peace Prize. His memoirs, a triple award-winning and critically acclaimed trilogy series of graphic novels recounting civil rights, titled "March," will stand as an enduring testament to his legacy (Lewis et al., 2020).

Lewis symbolized the highest expectation and durability, parting even in his days with a message for the future: "Get in good trouble; necessary trouble." His death became the loss of a hero, but what remained was the spirit and determination of non-violent protests that moved people around the world. John Lewis' legacy is a reminder that real potential lies in the ability of ordinary people to create extraordinary change and the necessity to fight for the right unbowed, however costly.

4. Jesse Jackson

Date of Birth: October 8, 1941

Date of Death: Jesse Jackson is alive as of 2025-01-02.

He was a prominent civil rights activist and a Baptist minister who worked alongside Martin Luther King Jr. and founded the Rainbow/PUSH Coalition to carry on that fight for justice.

The history of one of the most thumping personal eminences that America produced on the surface of civil rights, Jesse Jackson, had its roots in Greenville, South Carolina, where he was born on October 8, 1941. Jackson's life journey can be epitomized by an amalgamation of activism, leadership, and controversy from its inception in the civil rights movement.

Jackson would later be hammered into one of the most influential leaders of the University of Illinois and the Agricultural and Technical College of North Carolina. At the same time, Jackson's experiences in the civil rights movement—the Selma, Alabama, march with Dr. Martin Luther King, Jr.—were forever etched into his being.

In the late 1960s, he moved to Chicago and further entrenched himself on the path of activism and advocacy. In 1971, he set up People United to Save Humanity (Operation PUSH), which focused relatively well on black self-help and progressive issues (Phillip, 2023). His activism moved on to found the National Rainbow Coalition in 1984, championing the rights of oppressed communities.

Jackson ran in 1984 and 1988 presidential bids, seeming to run to become president eventually, and in so doing, won a substantial number of votes that broke new ground for political involvement by African Americans. After criticism and controversies through his connections to Louis Farrakhan and his incendiary statements often lampooned by contemporaries and pundits, including one about New York City as a "hymie town," Jackson stayed to be a great exponent of black uplift within the Democratic Party (Gibson, 2023).

Though all of these are purely his domestic issues, activism went way further than this. He was a chief negotiator for some international conflicts and a mighty fighter for human rights in South Africa and the Middle East (Dell'Omo, 2021). At the time, much was said by his critics, lauding his diplomatic work there and casting illumination on a deeper degree of resolve for global justice. His contributions inspire generations in the struggle for equality and social justice.

Civil Rights Martyrs

The names of those who died fighting for freedom in Alabama between February and August 1965—during the contemporary Civil Rights Movement—are inscribed on the landmark Civil Rights Memorial. Activists who were pursued for execution because of their civil rights activities, those who sacrificed their own lives to raise consciousness of the reason, and arbitrary victims of militants seeking to put an end to the movement are all considered martyrs. The lives of four people who were chosen at random throughout the specified timeframe are briefly described in the chronology below:

1. Rev. James Reeb March 11, 1965 · Selma, AL

Date of Birth: 1st January, 1927

Date of death: March 11, 1965

Unitarian Universalist minister Reeb was beaten and killed by white supremacists after participating in the Selma to Montgomery marches in Selma, Alabama.

One of the numerous white pastors who accompanied the Selma protesters following the state trooper attack at the Edmund Pettus Bridge was Rev. James Reeb, a Unitarian minister from Boston. Reeb was walking along a Selma street when he was assaulted to death by white males "("Civil rights martyrs," n.d.)."

2. Viola Gregg Liuzzo March 25, 1965 · Alabama's Selma Highway

Born: April 11, 1925

Date of Death: March 25, 1965

A white civil rights activist from Michigan, Liuzzo was murdered by Ku Klux Klan members while driving her fellow activists during the Selma-Montgomery marches.

When Detroit mother and homemaker Viola Gregg Liuzzo saw footage of the massacre at the Edmund Pettus Bridge on television, she decided to drive alone to Alabama to assist with the Selma march. When a Klansman fatally shot her in a passing car, she was transporting demonstrators between Selma and Montgomery "("Civil Rights Martyrs," n.d.)."

3. Jimmie Lee Jackson February 26, 1965 · Marion, Alabama

Birth Date: December 16, 1938

Death Date: February 26, 1965

An African American civil rights activist whose death at the hands of an Alabama state trooper inspired the Selma to Montgomery marches.

While attempting to save his mother and grandfather from a police onslaught on civil rights protestors, Jimmie Lee Jackson was shot and assaulted by state troopers. Following his passing, the Voting Rights Act was eventually passed, and the Selma–Montgomery march took place "("Civil Rights Martyrs," n.d.)."

17

4. Jonathan Myrick Daniels August 20, 1965 · Hayneville, Alabama

Birth Date: March 20, 1939

Death Date: August 20, 1965

An Episcopal seminarian and civil rights activist, Daniels was murdered in Hayneville, Alabama protecting a young Black girl from a shotgun blast.

A student at Boston Episcopal Seminary named Jonathan Myrick Daniels traveled to Alabama to assist with Lowndes County's black voter registration drive. He was taken into custody during a protest, imprisoned in Hayneville, and then unexpectedly freed. Shortly after being freed, a deputy sheriff shot and killed him "("Civil Rights Martyrs," n.d.)."

How "Bloody Sunday" in Selma Turned Into a Revolutionary Event in the Civil Rights Movement

The Voting Rights Act came forth partly as a result of the attack on civil rights demonstrators in Selma, Alabama. Alabama was still feeling the effects of slavery and Reconstruction's racial legacy in 1965, almost a century after the Confederacy's weapons were put down.

The world was startled by the footage of the brutality on March 7, 1965, when activist John Lewis, then 25 years old, led over 600 demonstrators through the Edmund Pettus Bridge in Selma, Alabama, and was brutally attacked by approaching state troopers. This incident sparked a national movement against racial discrimination. In some areas of the state, the historic Civil Rights Act of 1964, which was passed a few months prior, had not done much to guarantee African Americans' fundamental right to vote. In Dallas County, Alabama, where African Americans made up nearly fifty percent of the overall population but only 2 percent of voters who were registered, Jim Crow laws may have been enforced more strictly than anywhere else.

The Student Non-violent Coordinating Committee (SNCC) had faced months of setbacks in its attempts to register Black voters in Selma, the county seat. When Martin Luther King Jr. visited the city in January 1965, he announced that the Southern Christian Leadership Council (SCLC) supported the cause (Carson, 2005). Thousands were arrested due to non-violent protests in Selma and the neighboring towns. King, among others, wrote to the New York Times, "This is Selma, Alabama." More Black people are incarcerated with me than are registered to vote "(Racial Legislation, 2020)"

The murder of African American protestors in Marion by law enforcement officers.

On February 18, 1965, troopers from the state shot and killed 26-year-old Jimmie Lee Jackson, an African American protester attempting to shield his mother from being assaulted by police, after they clubbed protestors. This event marked the culmination of growing racial tensions that eventually burst into violence in the adjacent town of Marion (Romano, 2014).

In retaliation, civil rights activists intended to march 54 miles from Selma to Montgomery, the state capital, to directly confront Alabama Governor George Wallace. About 600 voting rights proponents marched on Sunday, March 7, despite Wallace's directive for state troopers "to adopt whatever tactics necessary to avert a march." The march began at the Brown Chapel AME Church.

King stayed in Atlanta with his religious group and intended to join the marchers the next day. King visited President Lyndon Johnson two days before to discuss voting rights reform. Lewis, a potential Georgia congressman and chairman of the SNCC, and Hosea Williams would coordinate the march on behalf of the SCLC; this was decided by a coin flip "("How Selma's 'Bloody Sunday' Became a Turning Point in the Civil Rights Movement," 2015)."

Protesters Cross the Edmund Pettus Bridge

Edmund Pettus Bridge is a historic bridge in Selma, Alabama, that was named after Edmund Winston Pettus, a Confederate general and U.S. Senator.

Birth: Construction started on 1939

The bridge took on a totally different meaning than it should have when "*Bloody Sunday*"-actions were recorded on March 7, 1965, where police brutally attacked peaceful protesters trying to march back to Montgomery.

The protesters marched peacefully across downtown Selma, where the past always lingered in the present. The marchers spotted Edmund Pettus, a prominent figure in the Alabama Ku Klux Klan and a Confederate general, on the crossbeam of the steel-arched bridge over the Alabama River. The name of Pettus was painted in large block letters and was visible to them as they crossed the bridge. Trouble was visible on the other side of the bridge as soon as Lewis and Williams crossed it. At the foot of the span, a wall of state troopers extended across Route 80, their hands pounding billy clubs while donning white helmets ("How Selma's 'Bloody Sunday' Became a Turning Point in the Civil Rights Movement," 2015). Following them were Jim Clark's county sheriff's officers, several of whom were mounted, and scores of white onlookers, many of whom were excitedly awaiting a confrontation while brandishing Confederate flags. The demonstrators continued in a narrow column along the sidewalk of the bridge, aware that a confrontation was imminent, until they came to a halt roughly fifty feet from the cops. Williams and Lewis held their ground at the front of the line. The troopers moved forward after a bit of a while, clubs ready and gas masks secured to their faces. They shoved Williams and Lewis away. The troopers then picked up their pace. They forced the protesters to the ground. They hit them with sticks. The applause of joyous onlookers blended with the scared marchers' screams when clouds of tear gas were released. As they swung clubs, whips, and rubber tubing wrapped in barbed wire, deputies on horseback surged forward, chasing the breathless men, women, and children back across the bridge. The demonstrators were forced back but did not resist ("Selma Campaign and the Voting Rights Act of 1965," 2020).

Lewis subsequently stated in court that after being knocked down, a state trooper struck him in the head with a nightstick. As Lewis attempted to stand up, the trooper struck him once more while Lewis covered his head with his palm.

A few weeks prior, King had chastised photographer Flip Schulke of Life magazine for not snatching away from demonstrators who police had knocked down but instead attempting to help them back up. Following the Pulitzer Prize-winning book The Race Beat, King told Schulke, "The entire world doesn't know this transpired because you failed to capture it." However, television cameras caught the whole attack this time, turning the small-town demonstration into a nationwide civil rights movement. The film was flown from Alabama to the television channel headquarters in New York over several hours. Still, the visuals and audio of "Bloody Sunday" horrified the American people when it was shown that night.

Nationwide indignation about "Bloody Sunday" spread. Protesters who supported the voting rights marchers organized protests, sit-ins, and traffic jams. Some even went to Selma, where two days later, King tried to march again, only to have troopers again block the highway at the Edmund Pettus Bridge, much to the chagrin of some protesters ("How Selma's 'Bloody Sunday' became a turning point in the civil rights movement," 2015).

Ultimately, on March 21, the voting rights marchers—protected by federalized National Guard troops—left Selma after a federal court order approved the demonstration. When they arrived in Montgomery four days later, the crowd had grown to 25,000 when they approached the capitol grounds. The Selma events compelled Congress to enact the Voting Rights Act, ratified by President Johnson on August 6, 1965. The bridge that was the setting for "Bloody Sunday" is today a significant historic civil rights landmark, even though it still carries the label of a white supremacist ("Civil rights movement," n.d.). The Edmund Pettus Bridge came to represent the profound shifts occurring in Alabama, the United States, and the global community. On March 7, 1965, law enforcement officers aggressively confronted voting rights protestors here. Bloody Sunday was the moniker given to the day.

Personal Note

Obtaining the right to vote was not an easy task.

Black people would discuss obtaining the right to vote at meetings and in churches. During black church meetings, three or four black people would hide in the woods with rifles, watching over the building to make sure white people set it on fire while they were inside.

Many Black individuals would visit the courts to register to vote, but none were successful.

Large numbers of Black people would occasionally travel to the courts to register to vote, where they would be subjected to irrational questioning to obtain the right to vote. They might be asked, for instance, how many jellybeans were in the jar. If they were correct, they would be allowed to register to vote; if they were wrong, they would be expelled.

My grandfather used to ferry a truckload of black folks back then to register to vote. For instance, when my grandfather took 15 to 20 individuals daily, the courthouse would either register one person or none. Frequently, the courthouse would dismiss everyone and declare that they were closed for the day.

#OnThisDay: Bloody Sunday

Image Credit:1965 Spider Martin

Bloody Sunday commemorates the anniversary of a march for the 600 victims of the Edmund Pettus Bridge attack that took place in Selma, Alabama, in 1965. There, law enforcement agents used billy clubs to beat defenseless protestors and doused them in tear gas ("#OnThisDay: Bloody Sunday," n.d.).

A black-and-white photograph of Amelia Boynton Robinson, who is weak from being attacked and gassed by Alabama State Troopers. Credit: © 1965 Spider Martin

State police from Alabama severely battered activist Amelia Boynton Robinson when she was participating in the march. The ferocity of the fight for African Americans' right to vote was depicted in this image, which brought the cause global attention. Working closely with Dr. Martin Luther King Jr. and the SCLC, Robinson was a key organizer of the march. Robinson had a long history of activity; from the 1930s to the 1950s, he organized African American registration drives for voters in Selma and co-founded the Dallas County Voters Alliance in 1933 ("#OnThisDay: Bloody Sunday," n.d.).

The Voting Rights Act was a significant federal victory of the 1960s Civil Rights Movement, enacted later that year ("#OnThisDay: Bloody Sunday," n.d.).

A black-and-white photograph of the March 7, 1965 assault on Civil Rights marchers by Alabama state police officers termed "Bloody Sunday." The troopers, wearing gas masks and brandishing nightsticks, set upon marchers along US Highway 80. Credit: © 1965 Spider Martin

History

President Barack Obama was born on August 4, 1961, in Honolulu, Hawaii.

Because of Bridge Crossing Jubilee, we could elect our first Black President. On November 4, 2008, President Barack Obama became the first African-American to be elected President. He resigned his seat in the U.S. Senate on November 16, 2008. Barack Obama was inaugurated as the 44th President of the United States on January 20, 2009.

Barack Obama was the first Black president of the United States of America from 2009 to 2017. His election marked a sea change in American politics and culture, a testament to how far the country had come on its long journey toward racial equality. The presidency opened more than doors; it let a message be said to the world, especially on the fringes, that, no dream is beyond reach (Thorn, 2021).

His early life, filled with global influences and academic rigor, formed his worldview about unity and inclusivity. As president, his leadership style would underscore diplomacy, healthcare reform, and efforts to bridge divides in a polarized political environment. Other notable accomplishments of his administration include the Affordable Healthcare Act, the elimination of Osama bin Laden, and serious progress with climate change (Bose & Fritz, 2024).

The Obama family always played an important role in humanizing presidencies. Michelle, the first Black First Lady, stands tall and extends her prowess in causes, including healthy living, education, and welfare for girls. Certainly, her call to action went way beyond the White House and helped create lasting change in how people empower them and continue to engage civically. The daughters of the Obamas, Malia, and Sasha, grew up in the limelight but with a sense of normalcy because of their parents' emphasis on privacy and family values that keep them grounded (Dodd, 2024).

28

The Obamas personified the new, relevant, aspirational American family. The love, warmth, and genuineness that bound them together as one echoed across the globe and largely explained their enduring appeal. Obama's presidency was as much a political victory as a cultural moment, underlining in indelible ink the possibilities of diversity and equality in leadership.

The First Black President is President Barack Obama

KAMALA HARRIS

Authored By: Iesha Shaw

Kamala Devi Harris

Born on the 20th of October 1964, Kamala Devi Harris is an American politician and lawyer who has been US vice president since 2021, working under President Joe Biden. Harris is the 2024 presidential candidate of the Democratic Party. She is the first Asian American, Black American, and woman to serve as the vice president, attorney general of California, and district attorney of San Francisco (Clayton et al., 2021). She is also the first woman of Afro-Jamaican and Tamil Indian heritage to serve in her position. She also served as California's representative in the US Senate from 2017 to 2021 (Lerer & Ember, 2020). In American history, she is the most senior female official. Harris, a native of Oakland, California, holds degrees from Howard University and Hastings College of the Law at the University of California (Ma et al., 2021). Her first legal job was at the Alameda County district attorney's office. After being recruited, she worked for the San Francisco District Attorney's Office and the city's attorney's office. She won the San Francisco district attorney's seat in 2003, the California attorney general's seat in 2010, and the attorney general's seat again in 2014 (Ma et al., 2021).

From 2017 until 2021, Harris served as California's junior US senator. She became the first South Asian American and the second Black woman elected to the US Senate in 2016 (Ma et al., 2021). Harris supported federal legalization of cannabis, the DREAM Act, stricter gun control legislation, and changes to taxes and healthcare while serving as a senator. Her incisive questions of Trump administration officials during Senate hearings, notably Brett Kavanaugh, Trump's second nomination for the Supreme Court, brought her widespread attention. In 2019 Harris entered the 2020 Democratic presidential candidacy but dropped out before the primaries (Lerer & Ember, 2020). Biden chose her as his running mate, and in the 2020 election, their ticket defeated incumbents Mike Pence and Donald Trump (Clayton et al., 2021). As Senate President, Harris was instrumental in overseeing an evenly divided Senate when she took office. More tie-breaking votes than any previous vice president were cast by her, assisting in passing legislation like the Inflation Reduction Act of 2022 and the American Rescue Plan Act of 2021 stimulus package (Stow, 2023). Harris started her campaign with Biden's support when he pulled out of the 2024 presidential contest. She selected Minnesota Governor Tim Walz as her running mate on the 6th of August, 2024.

Why is attending the Bridge Crossing Jubilee worthwhile?

A Living History

The Bridge Crossing Jubilee, a significant occasion honoring the Selma to Montgomery marches and the fight for voting rights in America, enables one to learn about the origins of the civil rights movement.

Connections

It's a fantastic way to connect with people from different backgrounds, making it perfect for activists, community leaders, and anybody looking to network and have deep conversations.

Fairness in Social Matters

For activists and advocates, it offers a unique opportunity to participate in conversations and events that center on current social justice issues while also finding inspiration in the history of the civil rights struggle.

The Landmark

The famous Edmund Pettus Bridge provides a sad and contemplative experience for those who appreciate American history. It is an emblem of the uphill battle and victory of the civil rights campaign.

Workshops

Educational excursions and conferences allow visitors to acquire insightful knowledge, making this a must-visit location for learners, teachers, and history buffs interested in learning about civil rights history.

Events & Shows of Cultural Interest

Taking part in various cultural events that honor the depth and diversity of Black culture is a great way to immerse oneself fully in African-American heritage.

References

- #OnThisDay: Bloody Sunday. (n.d.). National Museum of African American History and Culture. https://nmaahc.si.edu/explore/stories/onthisday-bloody-sunday

- Ball, H., & Horwitz, M. J. (2000). The Warren court and the pursuit of justice: A critical issue. The American Historical Review, 105(1), 251. https://doi.org/10.2307/2652539

- Brown v. Board of education: Summary, ruling & impact. (2009, October 27). HISTORY. https://www.history.com/topics/black-history/brown-v-board-of-education-of-topeka

- Carson, C. (2005). Between contending forces: Martin Luther King, Jr., and the African American freedom struggle. OAH Magazine of History, 19(1), 17-21. https://doi.org/10.1093/maghis/19.1.17

- Civil rights movement. (n.d.). Religion Past and Present. https://doi.org/10.1163/1877-5888_rpp_sim_05001

- Haines, H. H. (1995). Black radicals and the civil rights mainstream, 1954-1970. Univ. of Tennessee Press.

- How Selma's 'Bloody Sunday' became a turning point in the civil rights movement. (2015, March 6). HISTORY. https://www.history.com/news/selma-bloody-sunday-attack-civil-rights-movement

- Racial legislation. (2020). Justifying Injustice, 116-157. https://doi.org/10.1017/9781316671412.005

- Romano, R. C. (2014). Racial reckoning. https://doi.org/10.4159/9780674736177

- The Selma campaign and the Voting Rights Act of 1965. (2020). The Civil Rights Movement, 165-180. https://doi.org/10.1002/9781119414261.ch9

- The struggle for civil rights. (2023, March 21). Miller Center. https://millercenter.org/the-presidency/educational-resources/age-of-eisenhower/struggle-civil-rights

- Tyson, T. B. (1998). Robert F. Williams, "Black power," and the roots of the African American freedom struggle. The Journal of American History, 85(2), 540. https://doi.org/10.2307/2567750

- Vann R. Newkirk II. (2017, February 16). How 'The Blood of Emmett Till' still stains America today. The Atlantic. https://www.theatlantic.com/entertainment/archive/2017/02/how-the-blood-of-emmett-till-still-stains-america-today/516891/

- Williams, H. A. (2014). Epilogue. American Slavery: A Very Short Introduction, 115-118. https://doi.org/10.1093/actrade/9780199922680.003.0007

- https://www.google.com/url?sa=i&url=https%3A%2F%2Fpeople.com%2Fpolitics%2Fobama-family-photos-through-the-years%2F&psig=AOvVaw3NqVRY_ZQXhSw7Elte1aa5&ust=1718907692397000&source=images&cd=vfe&opi=89978449&ved=0CBMQjhxqFwoTCJC_r6Kl6IYDFQAAAAAdAAAAABAK

- https://www.obamalibrary.gov/obamas/president-barack-obama

- Bose, M., & Fritz, P. (Eds.). (2024). Evaluating the Obama Presidency: From Transformational Goals to Governing Realities (Vol. 1). Walter de Gruyter GmbH & Co KG.

- Dodd, S. (2024, November 1). All about Barack and Michelle Obama's 2 daughters, Malia and Sasha Obama. People.com. https://people.com/politics/all-about-barack-obama-michelle-obama-daughters/

- Thorn, K. D. (2021). How America's Racist History Affected Barack Obama's Movement as President of the United States (Master's thesis, University of Michigan-Flint).

Made in the USA
Middletown, DE
15 January 2025

69490095R00024